Little Night

YUYI MORALES

A NEAL PORTER BOOK
ROARING BROOK PRESS
NEW MILFORD, CONNECTICUT

As the long day comes to an end,
Mother Sky fills a tub with falling stars
and calls, "Bath time for Little Night!"
   Little Night answers from afar, "Can't
come. I am hiding and you have to find
me, Mama. Find me now!"

"Hmmm," Mother Sky looks down a rabbit hole. She puts her cheek on the darkest sand. When she peeks behind the hills, whom does she see?

"I found you, I found my
Little Night."
Face scrub, lather up, towel
spread, and catch Little Night
in the air.

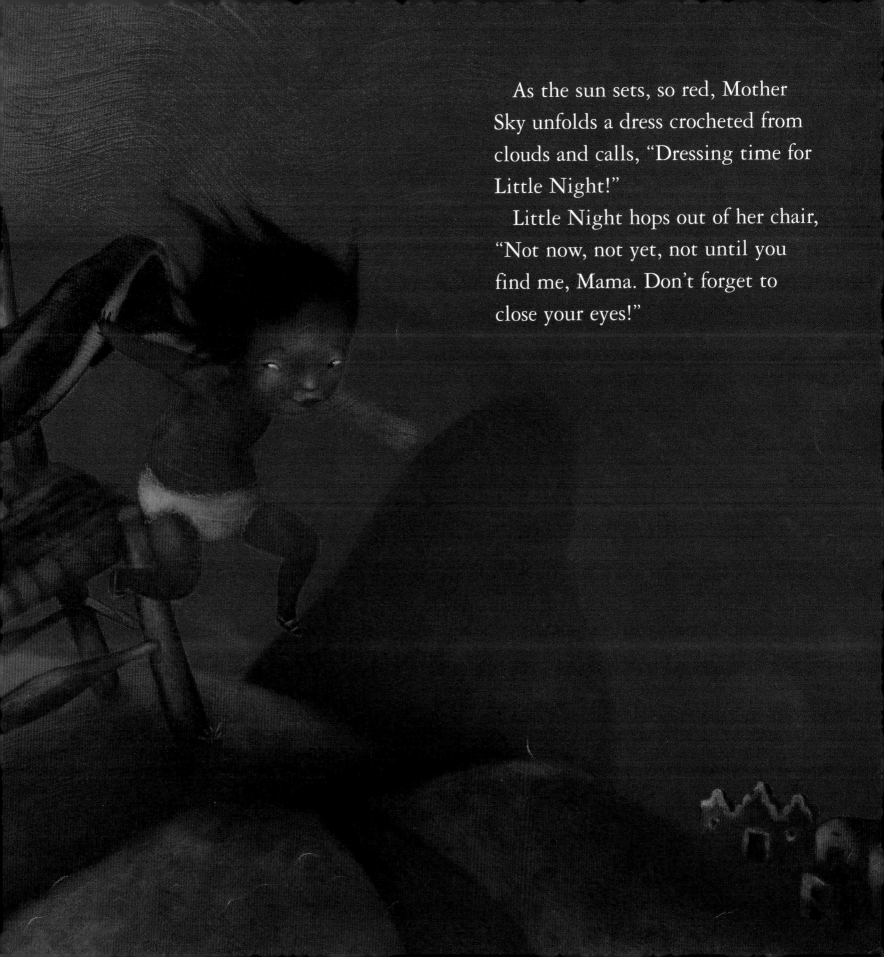

As the sun sets, so red, Mother
Sky unfolds a dress crocheted from
clouds and calls, "Dressing time for
Little Night!"

Little Night hops out of her chair,
"Not now, not yet, not until you
find me, Mama. Don't forget to
close your eyes!"

"Where could you be?"

Mother Sky hovers by the shade of trees. She searches in the stripes of bees. When she peeks inside the bats' cave, whom does she see?

"I found you, I found my
Little Night."
Two arms in, one head out,
button the white dress crocheted
from clouds.

As the warm of the day fades, Mother Sky
fills up a glass of milk and serves pancakes on
a plate. She calls, "Time to eat, Little Night!"

Little Night dashes past the table. "Count
first, Mama, from one to ten. It is going to
be hard to find me this time!"

Mother Sky counts, "One, two, three...
"Let's see," Mother Sky looks inside the
shuttered barn. She pats the raven chicks.
When she brushes her hand over the
blueberry field, whom does she see?

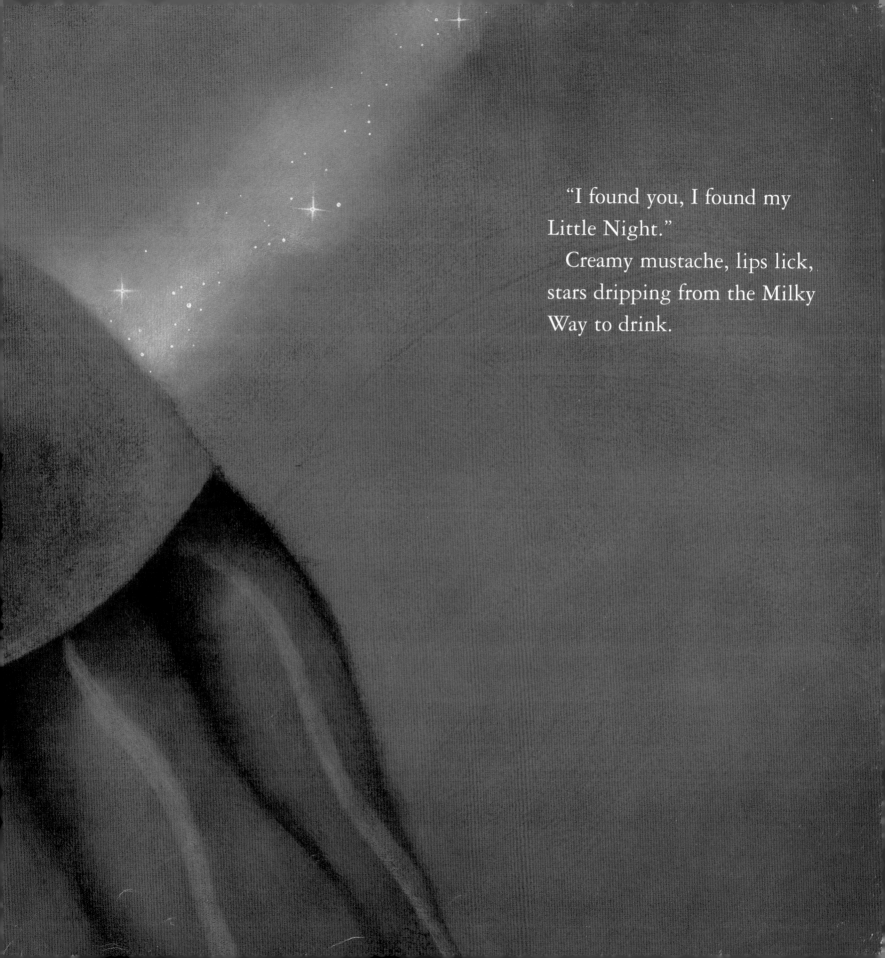

"I found you, I found my
Little Night."
   Creamy mustache, lips lick,
stars dripping from the Milky
Way to drink.

As fireflies and moths come out, Mother Sky
sits on her chair waving her comb. She calls,
"Time to comb your hair, Little Night."
But what does she hear? Only the hushing
of the balmy wind.

Mother Sky looks around, but Little Night is not peeking from behind the hills, nor is she hiding in the caves, nor vanishing into the field. "Where could my Little Night be?"

"Peekaboo, Mama.
I am right here!"

Mother Sky sits Little Night on her lap and with her shiny comb she untangles the knots, twists the hair between her fingers, and makes little swirls, one on the left side, one on the right.

To keep them in place
she takes three hairpins
from her pocket.
"Venus on the east,
Mercury on the west, and
Jupiter above."

"Now, my Little Night, take
your moon ball and play."
"I can catch it, Mama. See me
bounce it high into the air!"

In the flowered city there is an endless mother,
giving and magnificent like the sky.
She is my mother, Eloina. This book is for her.

Note: While making this book, I met two brave mothers, who, like many Mexican women,
are fighting cancer and poverty to keep alive. They have young children to love and raise,
and they work hard every day to stay with them. Señora Badillo y Asuncion, thank you for keeping me inspired.

Copyright © 2007 by Yuyi Morales

A Neal Porter Book

Published by Roaring Brook Press

Roaring Brook Press is a division of Holtzbrinck Publishing Holdings Limited Partnership

143 West Street, New Milford, Connecticut 06776

Distributed in Canada by H. B. Fenn and Company Ltd.

Library of Congress Cataloging-in-Publication Data:

Morales, Yuyi.

Little Night / written and illustrated by Yuyi Morales. — 1st ed.

p. cm.

"A Neal Porter Book."

Summary: At the end of a long day, Mother Sky helps her playful daughter, Little Night, to get ready for bed.

ISBN-13: 978-1-59643-088-4

ISBN-10: 1-59643-088-5

[1. Bedtime—Fiction.   2. Mothers and daughters—Fiction.   3. Night—Fiction.   4. Sky—Fiction.]

I. Title. II. Title: Nochecita.

PZ73.M7155 2006

[E]—dc22

2006011571

Roaring Brook Press books are available for special promotions and premiums.

For details contact: Director of Special Markets, Holtzbrinck Publishers.

First edition April 2007

Book design by Jennifer Browne

Printed in China

2 4 6 8 10 9 7 5 3 1